How do you like our book?

We would really appreciate you leaving us a review.

Other Picture Books:

For other fun Picture Books by Kampelstone,
simply search for:

Kampelstone Picture Books

FACTS ABOUT GERMANY

- Germany has the strongest economy in Europe.

- Germany was the first country to use Daylight Savings time.

- About two thirds of the German Autobahn has no speed limit.

- The world's first Green Political Party was founded in West Germany in 1980.

- Oktoberfest is the world's largest Volksfest (people's festival) and takes place during the last couple of weeks of September and the first few days of October.

- In fact, there is only one Oktoberfest in the world which is the yearly celebration in Munich, Germany. All other 'Oktoberfests' are knock-offs. In Munich, the event is not locally known as Oktoberfest but as d'Wiesn and is named after Theresienwiese, the fairgrounds where the two-week event takes place. It started when Therese of Saxe-Hildburghausen married Prince Ludwig of Bavaria on 12 Oct 1810. They sponsored a huge three day celebration in the fields just in front of Munich's city gates. These fields are now called Theresia's Meadow or Theresienwiese.

- The construction of the Cologne Cathedral (Kölner Dom) began in 1248. Construction was halted between 1560 and 1840 and altogether took some 700 years to build.

- The first book ever printed on a printing press was the Bible, printed in Mainz, Germany by Johannes Gutenberg in the 1450's. He originally printed 180 copies but only 48 still exist to this day.

- The longest word ever published in the German language is the 79 letter long word: Donaudampfschifffahrtselektrizitätenhauptbetriebswerkbauunterbeamtengesellschaft which means "Danube steamboat shipping electricity main engine facility building sub clerk association".

- The Berlin Wall was built in 1961 and fell in 1989.

- Munich hosted the Olympic games in 1972. During the games, the Israeli team was held hostage and eleven members were killed by terrorists.

- During his speech in Berlin in 1962, President Kennedy stated twice: "Ich bin ein Berliner".

- Germans are the third most efficient country in the world to recycle after Switzerland and Austria.

- Over the centuries, Germany has had seven capitals: Aachen from 794 – 814, Nuremberg 1536-1543, Regensburg from 1663-1803, Frankfurt-am-Main 1860-1866, Berlin 1871-1945, 1990 to present and Bonn from 1949-1990.

- The world's tallest cathedral is the Ulmer Münster with a height of 530 feet (161.53 meters).

- The world's two largest cuckoo clocks are in Schonach and Schonachbach, Black Forest. The cuckoo clock was invented in the 17th century. The world's largest cuckoo clock is in Triberg and has an 26 foot (8meter) long pendulum.

- Germany is the second largest exporter of automobiles in the world, after Japan,

- German is spoken by over 100 million people worldwide.

- Germany has more than 400 registered zoos, more than any other country in the world.

- Germany shares borders with nine other countries: Austria, Belgium, Czech Republic, France, Switzerland, Denmark, Luxembourg, Holland and Poland.

- Germany has more football (soccer) clubs than any other country in the world.

- Germany is the 5th largest country in Europe after Ukraine, France, Sweden and Spain.

- Angela Merkel, chancellor of Germany was ranked as the world's second most powerful person.

- Berlin is nine times larger than Paris.

- Every year, 5,500 bombs, left over from air raids, are found in Germany.

- Germans consume more pork than any other type of meat.

- Hugo Boss designed the Nazi uniforms.